CAGED

CAGED

Norah McClintock

orca soundings

ORCA BOOK PUBLISHERS

Library and Archives Canada Cataloguing in Publication

McClintock, Norah, author
Caged / Norah McClintock.
(Orca soundings)

Issued in print and electronic formats.
ISBN 978-1-4598-1499-8 (softcover).—ISBN 978-1-4598-1500-1 (pdf).—
ISBN 978-1-4598-1501-8 (epub)

I. Title. II. Series: Orca soundings
PS8575.C62C33 2017   jC813'.54   C2017-900866-8
C2017-900867-6

First published in the United States, 2017
Library of Congress Control Number: 2017933019

Summary: In this high-interest novel for teen readers,
Kenzie's dog is stolen by a dog-fighting operation.

*Orca Book Publishers is dedicated to preserving the environment and has
printed this book on Forest Stewardship Council® certified paper.*

Orca Book Publishers gratefully acknowledges the support for its
publishing programs provided by the following agencies: the Government
of Canada through the Canada Book Fund and the Canada Council
for the Arts, and the Province of British Columbia through
the BC Arts Council and the Book Publishing Tax Credit.

Edited by Tanya Trafford
Cover image by iStock.com and Shutterstock.com

ORCA BOOK PUBLISHERS
www.orcabook.com

Printed and bound in Canada.

20   19   18   17   •   4   3   2   1

Other Orca Soundings
by Norah McClintock

Chapter One

"Clancy! Come here, boy!"

Clancy was my dog. He was usually all over me when I was getting his breakfast, trying to weave in and out between my legs like a cat, the way he used to when he was small. Mostly he ended up with his snout in my crotch. It was as if he had no clue he wasn't a puppy anymore. He was an almost-full-grown chocolate Lab with the brain of a human toddler. He had a lot to learn, and mostly he learned the hard way, like the time he tried to take on the Taylors' cat and got clawed in the muzzle. Or last summer, when we took him camping and he met his first porcupine. You didn't want to mention vet bills around my parents for months after that.

Don't get me wrong, though. We all loved Clancy. He was a big, slob-bery, fun-loving mushy pooch, right up to the point where he sensed that any member of his pack (which consisted of my mom, my dad, my sister and me) was threatened in any way. He'd never bitten anyone. Never had to, really, not that he would. He was too gentle for that. But—and this is an important but—if Clancy didn't know you, and if he thought you were up in my face about something, you'd hear that snarl and you'd see those teeth—big teeth, sharp-looking teeth—and you'd back off. Chaz Rintoul backed off that time he thought he could shake me down for cigarette money. That guy who came around pretending to be from the gas company and insisting he had to see our water heater backed off so fast he almost fell down the porch steps. When my mom says no, she means no. When the guy didn't stop trying to strong-arm her, she looked down at the dog, who, of course, had wedged himself between her and the doorframe, and said, "Clancy." That's all it took. We were never bothered by phony gas-company guys after that.

"Clancy! Come on, boy!" I made a noisy job of adding water to the dried food I had already scooped into his bowl. You stirred the water in, and it made a sloppy, room-temperature gravy that Clancy slurped up as if it were the nectar of the gods.

Clancy didn't come running.

I set his food bowl on the plastic mat Mom insisted we use because Clancy was a messy eater. Then I went looking for him.

"Kenzie, please!" my mom called down from her room. "It's early!"

It was past nine o'clock. Most days of the week, Clancy would be the only one left in the house by nine. The rest of us would be at work or school. But this was Sunday. We were all home, and my parents always slept in on Sundays. I was going to have breakfast and then go meet my friends. I was going to take Clancy with me. He was cool to hang with my friends, and he never made any trouble, and if I had soccer practice, he flopped down on the sidelines and watched. He was just as patient when we played pickup softball. He never made a pain of himself or chased the ball unless I made it clear that it was playtime.

"Is Clancy up there with you?" I called to my mom.

I heard the upstairs bathroom door open. "He's in the backyard!" my sister, Traci, called down. "I let him out before my shower."

"That was nearly an hour ago," I said. I'd heard her go into the bathroom. I was surprised Clancy wasn't pawing at the door or barking to get back in so he could have breakfast. Clancy couldn't read a clock or a watch, but he always knew exactly when it was time to eat.

I went through the kitchen to the back porch, which was glassed in, and opened the door. "Clancy!" I shouted out into the yard. "Come on, boy!"

We have a big backyard. Everyone does around here, except for the people

who live right downtown. The houses
at our end of town are all medium-
sized but sit on big properties. They
were built when people started moving
here because there were good jobs in
a couple of canneries and at a nuclear
power plant that started up back in the
sixties. The canneries shut down when
I was a baby. The nuclear power plant
was decommissioned two years ago.
Then the town morphed into a bedroom
suburb, a place people move to when
they don't want to live in the city and
don't mind the three-hour round-trip
commute five days a week. Believe
it or not, there are people like that
around. So many, in fact, that new sub-
divisions were built at the other end of
town—massive houses in tiny postage-
stamp-sized yards.

Our yard was fenced in, so I wasn't
worried about Clancy. But I was curious

why he hadn't answered me. What was he up to?

"Clancy! Come on, boy!"

He still didn't come. And I couldn't see him anywhere.

I went down the porch steps and around to the other side of the yard, calling his name.

Nothing.

I started getting a little scared. I walked all around the house and right to the trees at the back of the yard. I checked the fence while I was at it. It was solid. There was no way anything could have got through. Was there? And there was no way Clancy would have jumped over it. He knew better than that.

So where was he?

I ran back inside just long enough to (1) chew out my sister for leaving Clancy outside so long, (2) tell my mom what had happened and (3) grab my jacket. Then I got my bike out of the garage and started pedaling around the neighborhood, calling Clancy's name.

I didn't see him. He didn't answer. And he didn't come running. Now I was really worried.

I stopped whenever I saw someone outside—a man raking leaves, a woman digging in a flower bed (even though everything in it looked dead to me), some kids skateboarding on hilly Broad Street. No one had seen a chocolate Lab.

"I heard there's lots of dogs going missing lately," one of the skater kids said. He looked about twelve. So did his buddies.

"There's always dogs missing," another kid said. "My dad says it's because people up here let their dogs run free." He was one of the new ones who had moved up from the city.

"He says coyotes and bears and wolves probably get them."

"Clancy was in our yard. It's fenced in." I don't know why, but I wanted these kids to know that I looked after my dog. I didn't let him run free unless I was with him, and he was trained to return when I whistled. He did it every time.

"The fence can't be all that good if your dog got out," the first kid said.

"There's nothing wrong with the fence." Besides checking the fence, I had checked the gate. I don't know why it took so long for the big question to occur to me, but it finally did. If the gate was locked and there were no holes in the fence and no place where a dog might have dug under it, then how did Clancy get out of the yard?

Had someone let him out?

Why would anyone do something so dumb?

Chapter Two

I rode all over town, shouting until my throat began to hurt. But no sign of Clancy. I headed home.

My mom was all over me the second I came through the side door. "Did you find him? Where is he?"

"I don't know," I said.

"What? No Clancy?" That was my dad. He appeared from behind my mom,

a mug of coffee in one hand, the news-
paper in the other. It's what my dad did
on Sundays. He drank coffee and read
the papers all morning, every section,
like he was training to be a contestant
on *Jeopardy!*

"I couldn't find him anywhere, Dad.
It's like he vanished."

"Nonsense," my dad said. "A dog
that size?" He handed my mom his mug
and paper. "Come on, I'll get the car.
We'll take another look."

We drove all over town. We crept
down alleys and even drove up and
down the county road as slowly as my
dad dared. "I can't imagine what he'd
be doing way out here," my dad said.
We came up empty.

I couldn't help it. I felt burning hot
tears in the corners of my eyes. I fought
them back, but there was nothing I could
do about the lump in my throat and the
sick feeling in my stomach.

"Where could he be?" I said. "He's never run away before. Why would he run away now? And how did he get out of the yard?"

"That is the jackpot question," my dad said. "Although, frankly, the point is moot. The horse is out of the barn, so to speak. Doesn't matter how it happened. All that matters is we get him back. Right, son?"

"Right."

My dad had a plan. "We'll make flyers," he said. "With a picture. We'll post them all over town. We can get that done today. I know Reg will let us use his photocopier."

Reg was one of my dad's poker buddies. He ran a real estate office in town.

"And we'll call the SPCA," my dad added.

"The nearest one is over in Apsley," I said.

"I know it's unlikely that anyone has picked him up already and taken him there. But we have to check. What if he was hurt?"

"But he was wearing his collar. He had tags."

"I don't know what to tell you, Kenz," my dad said. "We've got to try all the possibilities." I knew he was as worried as I was. "I don't get it," he added. "This isn't like Clancy at all."

My mom put together a flyer with a picture of Clancy and the words *Lost Dog. Chocolate Lab. Answers to Clancy. Friendly. Reward offered.* She included our phone number and her cell number. Dad called Reg, who unlocked his office for us and told us to make as many copies as we wanted. He gave us a tape gun too, so that we could plaster the town with our flyers.

It took most of the day to tape up the posters so that everyone in town would have a chance to see one. We talked to people too, but no one had seen Clancy. One man mentioned that a neighbor of his had lost her dog a few months back.

"Animal just disappeared," he said. "Like aliens abducted him. She never saw him again. No one did."

I felt those hot tears again. This time I had to turn away to wipe them before anyone saw. Wherever Clancy was, I hoped he was safe. I hoped he wasn't hurt. I was pretty sure he was hungry, but there was nothing I could do about that until I found him.

Dad drove us back home. I had schoolwork to do. It was hard to concentrate. I kept listening for Clancy and staring out my window into the backyard, even when it was too dark to see much.

Mom usually insisted on what she calls an old-fashioned Sunday dinner.

We always ate it in the dining room instead of the kitchen, and she put a tablecloth on the table instead of place mats. Plus she usually made a dessert from scratch. My favorite was pie. Any kind. But the day Clancy disappeared, Mom said she didn't feel like cooking. We had a barbecued chicken from the supermarket instead, with a little bucket of roasted potatoes and another of coleslaw. We all picked at our food. Maybe we were all thinking the same thing—if Clancy were here, he would have been skulking around the table, looking up at us with his pathetic begging eyes. Sunday dinner didn't seem right without him. Nothing did.

"We're not giving up," Dad said finally. "We're going to keep looking. Clancy isn't just a good dog. He's a member of this family. Besides, he can't have gone far."

"How did he even get out of the yard?" I asked. "There's nothing wrong with the fence. I checked."

"Maybe he jumped over it," Traci said. She's a year younger than me and some kind of genius. My teachers all wonder how she could have a big brother like me. You could say I'm not the academic type. That's fine with me. I want to get into the trades, like my uncles Jim and Dan. They're Mom's brothers. Uncle Jim is an electrician and owns his own company. So does Uncle Dan, who's a plumber. Both of them have pretty sweet lives. Both have already told me they'll take me on as an apprentice and teach me the business from the ground up.

I looked at my sister. I couldn't believe she had said something so dumb. "Clancy doesn't jump over fences," I said.

"Maybe he saw a squirrel. He'll do anything when he sees a squirrel."

"He would have come back." That was what bothered me. If Clancy had somehow turned into Superdog and leaped over the fence in a single bound, he would have come back. Maybe not right away, but for sure he would have been back in time for supper. Clancy wasn't an adventurer. He never looked for trouble. He'd learned to wait until his leash snapped into place before he headed for the door. In the two years we'd had him, he'd calmed down from the wild puppy who chewed everything from shoes to woolen mittens and who jumped up on everyone all the time. "What do you think happened to him, Dad?"

My dad shook his head. "I wish I knew, Kenzie. It's a real mystery."

After supper I texted all my friends and let them know that Clancy was missing.

They all promised to keep an eye out for him. I wanted to go out again and look around. At first Mom said no, because I had school the next day. But a few minutes later my dad poked his head into my room and said, "One more look around before bedtime won't hurt."

We drove all around town again, but we didn't find Clancy.

It felt all wrong going to bed without him. Clancy's bed was in the kitchen. He was supposed to sleep there. But he always snuck up to my room and bunked down on the floor beside my bed. At least, he started out on the floor. Usually he jumped onto the bed when I was asleep, so that whenever I turned over in the night, I found myself nose to nose with a big brown dog. Funny how you get used to things like that.

I had trouble lying still in bed that night, never mind falling asleep. I kept worrying about Clancy. It was late

October already, and it got cold at night. Frost-producing cold, so that when you got up in the morning, the lawn was covered with a skin of white that turned to glittering drops of water when the sun came out. Even if Clancy found shelter under someone's porch or maybe in a garage someone had left open, he would be cold all night. He wasn't used to that. He was used to sneaking into my room and snuggling next to me on my bed.

He was probably hungry too. We fed him in the morning and at suppertime. We all snuck him a treat now and then. But the last time I had given him anything to eat was over twenty-four hours ago, when I'd fed him supper. He hadn't even had his breakfast today. I hoped he had managed to find something to eat. The thought of him starving as well as freezing made me want to cry.

Maybe he was hurt. That was the worst thought, and the one I had trouble shaking. Clancy was a smart dog. He'd lived with us since he was old enough to be separated from his mother. He knew the neighborhood. He knew the town. He had a dog's sense of smell, which is a million times more powerful than a human's. He could find his way home.

So why hadn't he?

Had something happened to him? Had he wandered out to the highway and been hit by a car? Was he lying injured by the road somewhere? Was he in pain? Was he scared? Was he—I couldn't even think the word—was he gone forever? It was so terrible to think about. I couldn't imagine life without Clancy.

Chapter Three

Clancy whimpered in the darkness. He had been out in the yard, relieving himself, when he saw the meat. Right there. Right in the yard. He ate it. It tasted so good, especially since he was already hungry for breakfast. That was all he remembered until he woke up. He didn't know where he was, but he knew he wasn't at home.

He had woken up in a small space. A box with a door with metal bars on it. But it wasn't the cramped box or the inky darkness that made Clancy whimper with fear. It was the smells all around him, and what they told him.

He smelled food. Meat. Not the kind of meat that Kenzie put in his bowl sometimes. Not the kind of meat that Kenzie and sometimes Traci slipped him under the table—cooked meat, delicious and juicy. No, what he smelled was the meat before it went into the oven. Raw meat. Fresh meat, because he smelled blood too. At first the smell made him crazy with hunger. He barked, *Where's mine? Where's mine?*

A man came and opened the box and jerked him out of it. He beat Clancy and told him to shut up. Then he shoved him back into the box and closed the door. No food appeared.

He smelled other animals too. Dog. Lots of dogs. And some of what he smelled made him nervous. He heard barking and growling. He heard a clinking sound too, like metal on metal.

He smelled other animals besides the dogs. Squirrels and rabbits. Raccoons. They were all close by. He could tell that too. The thought excited him, and he barked again, but he stopped as soon as he smelled the man.

He hunkered down as best he could in the little space. His body was much too big for it, and his legs got sore after a little while. He shifted and tried to get comfortable. He lay with his chin on the ground between his front paws, with his nose pointed toward the door. When he closed his eyes, he saw the big bed with the dark-blue cover where Kenzie slept. He slunk up onto the bed every night and plastered himself against the warmth of Kenzie's body, and he fell asleep with the boy's smell filling his senses. He wished he were there now. He wished he were at home.

Chapter Four

I got up early the next morning and tiptoed downstairs to the front door.

"Great minds think alike," said a voice behind me.

I spun around. "Dad, you startled me."

My dad stood in the doorway to the kitchen. He had a mug of coffee in his hand and was already dressed for work, except for his tie. He only put that on after he had eaten his breakfast.

"I came down to do the same thing you're doing," he said. "To see if Clancy came back in the night. But he didn't. I checked the yard. I checked the neighbors' yards too."

"What do you think happened to him, Dad? Where is he? Why doesn't he come home?"

"The answer to all three of those questions is, I don't know. I wish I did, Kenzie. All we can do is keep looking and keep putting up posters so that if anyone finds him, they'll know who he belongs to."

Clancy had been missing for almost twenty-four hours. I finally said what I'd been afraid to even think ever since he'd gone missing.

"What if he doesn't come back, Dad?"

My dad squeezed my shoulder. "What do you say we cross that bridge when we come to it?"

Everyone at school who knew Clancy and knew he was missing asked me if I had found him yet. When I said no, they all promised to look for him. They meant well. But I couldn't stop worrying about where Clancy was and, even more important, *how* he was. Something had to be stopping him from coming home. But what?

I met my friends Ben and Jamal in the cafeteria at lunch as usual. But there was nothing usual about my appetite. My mom had packed me a sandwich, but after one bite I wasn't hungry anymore.

"Aren't you going to eat that?" Jamal asked. His eyes were all over my sandwich. My mom made good ones, and he knew it. I pushed it across the table to him. Jamal was big for his age—a whole head taller than Ben and half a head taller than me. He was bulky. He was an unstoppable force when we played football, mostly because he could knock the rest of us off our feet as if we were bowling pins and he was king of the lanes.

"I bet someone has found him by now," Ben said. "He was wearing his collar, right? He had tags, right? Either that or someone is going to see one of those posters you put up. He can't just disappear into thin air."

Ben always thought things were going to turn out okay. Maybe that was because he was a real brain in school. And because his dad was the head doctor at the regional hospital and had gone to one of the best schools in the country. He expected Ben to do the same. If Ben and I hadn't been best friends since kindergarten, I doubted we'd be friends now. He was as different from me as a purebred is from a mutt.

"He could vanish though," Jamal said through a mouthful of sandwich. "Say some truck hit him—say it was a semi. And say it threw him clear off the road. So it's possible no one will find him until one day someone stumbles across some bones—ow!" He shot a sharp look at Ben. Ben looked back at him evenly. "Oh," Jamal said. "Hey, sorry, Kenz. I was just talking theoretically. I didn't mean—"

"It's okay," I said. There was a huge lump in my throat, and it was hard to get the words out. "I've been thinking the same thing."

Jamal's eyes shifted to something behind me. Ben turned to look.

Then someone said, "I heard your dog is missing."

I twisted around in my chair. It was Gayle Worthington.

Gayle was short. Really short, like a little kid. She had a big nose, and she wore thick glasses. She wasn't popular. You never saw her hanging around with other girls. She was always on her own. A lot of people thought she was weird. A lot of other people, like me, didn't think about her at all. But here she was, talking to me.

Worse. Pulling out the chair next to mine and sitting down beside me.

"What happened?" she asked. "How did he disappear?"

"What's it to you?" Jamal asked. He didn't even try to be nice to her.

She turned to look at him. If his tone of voice bothered her, she didn't show it.

"Do you have a dog?" she asked.

"No," Jamal said.

"Then obviously I'm not talking to you." She turned to me again. "What happened?"

"He was out in the yard. When I went to call him, he was gone," I said.

"How long was he out there?"

"Maybe an hour. It was my sister who let him out, not me. I didn't even know he was out there."

"So no one was watching him?" Gayle asked.

I started to get mad. Why was she asking all these questions? Why was she making me feel as if I had done something wrong?

"Was the gate open?" she asked. "Was there a hole in the fence?"

"Look, what's with all the questions?" I demanded. "I don't even know you. Not really."

I thought that would make her get up and go away. It didn't.

"My dog disappeared two months ago," she said. "He was out in the yard, same as your dog. Only it was during the day. My mom lets him spend most of the day out in the yard if it's a nice day, and it was. It was a really nice day. She put him out while I was at school, and when I came home that day, he was gone. Our yard is fenced, and it's a high fence. And Pucci is a small dog. The gate is always locked. But he disappeared."

"And you haven't seen him since?" I didn't like the sound of that.

"That's not all," Gayle said. Her eyes, hazel with flecks of blue in them, swam behind her thick glasses. "I've been keeping track. In the past eight months, nearly sixty dogs have gone missing in town."

"Sixty? Is that a lot?" Jamal asked.

Ben shot him an annoyed look. "It sounds like a lot, doesn't it?"

"It is when you know in all of last year only twenty-two dogs went missing," Gayle said.

I thought about what one of the skateboarders had said. He'd heard that a lot of dogs had gone missing.

"All of them were found eventually," Gayle continued. "Most made their way home. One was hit up on the highway. But I can't find out anything about most of the ones that have gone missing this year." She paused, then asked, "So was there a hole in your fence? Was the gate unlocked?"

I shook my head. "That's the thing. I checked. The gate was closed, the fence is fine. I can't figure out how he got out."

"I've been to the police," Gayle said. "But they won't do anything."

"What do you mean they won't do anything?" Jamal asked. "What are the cops supposed to do about missing dogs?

They're not dogcatchers." He shot me a look, like he wished she would go away.

"Don't you get it?" Gayle said.

"Get what?" Jamal asked. "What do you think you know that we don't know? I'm dying of suspense." He looked more like he was dying of boredom.

Gayle ignored him.

"Most of the missing dogs vanished like Pucci and your dog. They vanished out of people's backyards."

"So?" I said.

She gave me a sad look, as if I had disappointed her.

"I think someone has been kidnapping dogs," Gayle said. "And when they take the dogs, they take them for good. Not a single one has been found."

Chapter Five

Clancy shivered. The nights had grown chilly now that it was autumn, and he was used to snuggling up to Kenzie's warm body on his big bed. His belly ached too. Although he smelled meat all around him, he had been given no food all day. Now it was dark. Clancy knew what that meant. It meant there would be no food for a long time, not until it got light.

He slept fitfully until a snarl jarred him awake. The minute he opened his eyes, he felt afraid. Where was he? Where was Kenzie? He heard another noise too. A scrabbling sound, with a strange scent to go with it. An animal scent. The other dogs must have smelled it too, because suddenly the air was filled with barking. Claws tore at metal bars. The barking went on for a long time and then faded away. Clancy put his head back down and whimpered.

He was wakened a second time by more barking, followed by the voice of a man. Clancy smelled food. Excitedly, he stretched his long limbs as much as he could in the small box. He pressed his nose against the metal bars of his prison door. Saliva pooled on the rough bottom of the box under his muzzle. The man was getting closer. The food smells were getting stronger. Clancy's whole body fluttered with anticipation.

Finally the man was standing in front of Clancy's box. He bent down a little and pressed an oily face close to the bars. Clancy smelled food and tobacco and man. Sour man.

"You hungry, boyo?" the man said. "I bet you are. And I got something for you, you bet I do. Soon. Real soon."

He laughed and walked away without giving Clancy anything to eat.

Chapter Six

"That's just plain dumb," Jamal said. "Why would anyone steal sixty dogs? What do you think this is? *101 Dalmatians*? You think someone is going to make a coat out of all those missing dogs?"

"That's not funny, Jamal," I said. What if some kind of crazy person had gotten hold of Clancy? What if he got his kicks torturing animals? They said Jeffrey Dahmer started that way, and he ended up as a serial killer.

"You care about your dog, right?" Gayle asked me.

"Of course I do!" I was insulted that she even had to ask. I cared about Clancy practically more than I cared about anything else.

"So help me find out what's going on. Help me find the missing dogs."

Jamal exploded with laughter. "The man's got better things to do than hang out with you," he said.

I knew exactly what he was thinking. Who in their right mind would want to hang around with a weirdo like Gayle Worthington? Except, if you asked me, she seemed to know what she was talking about.

"How do you know all those other dogs vanished out of people's yards?" I asked.

Gayle reached into a satchel, which I hadn't even noticed before, and pulled out a sheaf of papers, some of them wrinkled, most of them with pieces of tape still sticking to them. They looked like lost-animal posters. She slapped them down on the table in front of me. I was right. They were all lost-dog posters. There was even one of the ones I had put up about Clancy.

"I called every single one of these people," Gayle said, thrusting a finger at the top poster, where both a cell number and a landline number were listed. "Every single dog was taken from a yard, a car or a garage. Every single one."

"Fenced yards?"

"Fenced yards. And locked cars—not that those are hard to open with the right tool. The two that were in garages—those weren't locked. But it's not like the dogs could open the garage doors.

Someone is going to a lot of trouble to kidnap dogs around here."

"But why? What would anyone want with sixty dogs?" I asked.

Ben finally chimed in. "You said you went to the cops. What did they say?"

"They said that dogs go missing all the time. They also said that most of the owners hadn't even contacted them. They did the same thing I did. They put up posters. They called the SPCA. They checked the highways. They don't seem to think it's at all strange that not a single one of those dogs ever showed up. If you ask me, they just don't care."

"So what do you want Kenzie to do about it?" Jamal asked.

It was an excellent question.

"How are you planning to find the dogs when no one else has been able to so far?" I asked. "What are you going to do? Stake out all the backyards in town that have dogs in them and hope to catch the kidnappers in the act?"

"We could stake out a dog each," Gayle said.

"That's not going to help me find Clancy," I replied.

"If I'm right, you're never going to find him. The best you'll be able to do is find the dognappers."

I hated the way she kept saying that Clancy was a goner just because her dog hadn't come home again. She didn't know the first thing about Clancy.

I stood up abruptly. "Sorry, I have to get my math homework done. I want to look for Clancy after school. Are you guys going to help me?"

Of course they were. They were my best buddies. We left Gayle in the cafeteria and went to get our math out of the way.

After school we rode up to the highway. I still couldn't shake the idea that Clancy hadn't come home because he wasn't able to. Because he had been hurt. Maybe because he'd been hit by a car.

We rode a mile or so out on the county road, leaned our bikes by the fence on the far side of the culvert and started walking, two of us on one side of the road, one on the other, searching the tall grass, the culvert and the scrub beyond for any sign of Clancy. We'd been at it for nearly an hour when Ben shouted.

Jamal and I turned. Ben was holding something in his hand. It glinted in the sun, which was getting low in the sky.

"What is it?" Jamal asked.

Ben dropped what he had found into my hand. The blue metal tag in the shape of a dog's paw had Clancy's name engraved on it, plus our phone number. It was usually fastened to his collar by a metal ring, together with his other tags. But the ring for this tag was missing.

Ben opened his other hand. In it was a small metal ring. It looked exactly like the one that used to attach Clancy's tag to his collar. It had been pried open.

"Where did you find this?" I demanded.

Ben showed me. "It was right there." He pointed to a spot in the gravel on the shoulder of the road. Right beside it, tire tracks were still visible in the dirt, as if someone had pulled over.

I spun around and scanned the horizon. We were far enough out of town that all I saw were farmers' fields and scraggly bushes. In the distance, at least a quarter of a mile apart, were two farmhouses set on gentle rises far back from the road.

"You guys look here. Check every inch. See what else you can find." I started for my bike.

"What are you going to do?" Jamal asked.

"I'm going to check out those farm-houses and see if anyone saw anything."

I left Ben and Jamal to look around. I rode to the first farm and spoke to the owner, who was coming out of his barn about the time I reached his yard.

"Have I noticed anything?" he said, echoing my question. "Like what?"

"Anything unusual," I said. "Anyone hanging around by the side of the road over there. Any dogs."

"Dogs? What would dogs be doing over there?"

He hadn't seen anything. Worse, he seemed to think my question was completely weird. It shook me up so that I didn't have much confidence when I knocked on the door of the second house a few minutes later.

A woman answered the door. "Are you selling something? Because if you are…"

"I'm not selling anything. I lost my dog, and I just found one of his tags on

the other side of the road down there."
I pointed to where Ben and Jamal were
searching. "I was wondering if you've
seen anything unusual around here
lately."

"Unusual? You mean, like, your
dog?"

"Or maybe a strange car parked on
the side of the road," I said.

She thought for a moment.

"Well, there was that van," she said
slowly.

"What van?"

"A dark-blue van. At least, it looked
dark blue, but I guess that could have
been a trick of the light. Maybe it was
black. For sure it was dark-colored. It
was a dark-colored van."

"And it was parked over there?"

"Yes. A couple of times. The first
time I saw it, I thought maybe the driver
was lost or his vehicle had broken
down. I was half expecting him to show

up at my door and ask to use my phone. But I guess people don't do that anymore. I guess these days everyone has a cell phone."

"When was the last time you saw this van?" I asked.

"Not long ago. Maybe a day or two. Before that it was a couple of weeks at least. Maybe longer."

"You didn't happen to see the license plate, did you? Even just a few numbers."

The woman looked at me like I was crazy. "Honey, I couldn't see that far in my prime, and that was some time ago."

I thanked her and headed back to Ben and Jamal. By the time I got to where I'd left them, they were sitting on the fence side of the ditch, relaxing. Ben jumped to his feet when he saw me.

"We didn't find anything," he said. "How about you?"

"A woman over there says she saw a dark-blue van here a couple of times. Or maybe it was black. She's sure it was a dark color."

Jamal groaned. "That's no help at all."

"Maybe," I said. "Maybe not."

"What do you mean?" Ben asked. "What are you going to do?"

Chapter Seven

Clancy cowered when the man came back. He was torn between wanting to press himself against the back of his box and coming forward in hope of finally getting something to eat.

The sour-smelling man opened the door to Clancy's box. He reached in and dropped something over Clancy's head and around his neck. It was cold and thick and heavy. It clanked when Clancy moved. The man coiled one end of the thick chain around one of his hands. He smiled when he jerked on it. He jerked Clancy clean out of the box. Clancy tried to land on his feet, but they were numb from being cramped all night. He fell to the floor with a heavy thump.

The man got angry when Clancy fell. Clancy smelled his rage. It was even more bitter than his sour scent. Bitter and sharp, something you spit out if you ate it by mistake because you knew that taste could kill you. Clancy smelled it all over the man. He was so afraid that he cowered in front of the man even before the man started to beat him.

After the man beat Clancy and kicked him, he attached the end of the chain to a metal pole. The chain was heavy around Clancy's neck, and his neck was sore from the sour man's jerking on the chain.

His sides hurt where the man had kicked him. His head was cut and hurt from the beating the man had given him with a thick stick.

A terrible fear gripped the dog. From deep in his memory he dragged up one memory in particular—a memory of being beaten, before he went to live with Kenzie. Clancy curled himself into a ball. He trembled all over.

Chapter Eight

As soon as I got back to town, I went to the police station. Ben and Jamal came with me, but the sergeant at the desk made them wait out front while I talked to a plainclothes officer who didn't seem all that interested in what I had to say. He barely looked at Clancy's tag.

"So you're telling me that you think the driver of this dark-colored van has your dog? Is that it?" he asked when I had finished my story.

"That has to be it," I said. "How else did Clancy's tag get way out there? It looks like it was pried off." I showed him the little metal ring that had attached the tag to Clancy's collar. "Clancy couldn't have taken it off by himself."

"Maybe it was loose. Maybe it fell off," the officer said. "Or it got caught on something—a fence, maybe—and it got pulled off. There are lots of ways that tag could have come off."

"I think someone took my dog and took that tag off and threw it away. I think that person still has my dog. You have to find him."

"You think it was the owner of the dark-colored van?" he asked.

"Yes! So are you going to go out there and look?" I asked. "I can show you exactly where we found the tag."

"What do you think I should look for?" the officer asked.

"Clues. There are tire tracks. I'm pretty sure they belong to the van."

"Pretty sure?"

"You could find the van by matching its tire tracks." I'd seen that done on TV a hundred times.

"In the first place," the officer said, "do you have any idea how many dark-colored vans there are in town? Or how many pass through on the county road in the course of a week? What am I supposed to do? Ask every van owner in a fifty-mile radius to let me examine his tires? And then try to match those against tire tracks that you don't even know belong to a van?" He shook his head. "In the second place," he said, "I haven't heard any evidence that your dog was stolen. It sounds to me like you left him outside and he ran away. Was he outside when he disappeared?"

"I already told you. He was in the yard."

"*Was* is right. Then he got out."

"There was a van stopped by the side of the road the day that Clancy disappeared. That woman from the farm saw it. She saw it once before, parked in the same place. There are tire tracks in that place. It's also where I found Clancy's tag. That has to mean something. Can't you just go out there and look? Maybe there are other clues. Maybe—"

"Sorry, kid. I'm sorry about your dog. But we have real crimes to solve. You should talk to the SPCA. Maybe someone has brought in your dog by now."

"I already checked."

He stood up, my clue that he wanted me to leave.

"I hope you find him," he said. "If he's as smart as you say, he'll eventually come home. If he's able to."

That was the part that freaked me out—*if he was able to*. What if he wasn't able to? What if he was hurt? What if he was sick? What if he was hundreds of miles away by now?

"If you come up with something definite, let me know," the officer said.

Jamal and Ben went home for supper. I did the same, except that it took me twice as long as usual. That's because I rode around downtown first, looking for navy-blue vans. Or black ones. Or dark-colored ones. There were dozens, all makes and models. All different shades of dark too. Some were driven by women, some by men. Some were filled with kids or shopping or equipment. Some were parked in driveways, some were in parking lots, and some were on the street. Some even had dogs in them—the family pet.

I hated to admit it, but that cop had a point. Especially when there was nothing to even say that the van the woman saw was owned by someone in town. I felt sick inside. I hoped whoever had taken Clancy wanted him for a pet and would treat him well. But what if I was wrong?

Gayle said that sixty dogs had gone missing so far this year, three times as many as the previous year. She also said that none of the sixty dogs had ever been seen again. None of them had found their way home or been taken to the SPCA or been found by someone who had seen a missing-dog poster. They had simply vanished. What if that was because something bad had happened to them? Something very bad.

That night was even worse than the night before. I couldn't stop thinking about Clancy. We had gotten him from the SPCA in the first place. He had been found at a puppy mill, a terrible place where a so-called breeder was forcing dogs to have litter after litter of puppies. He didn't care if the mothers were healthy. He didn't care much about the babies either. He just wanted to get rid of them as soon as possible for as much money as possible. But nobody had wanted Clancy because he walked funny. It turned out one leg was a little shorter than the other. But that didn't matter to us.

The SPCA woman had warned us that Clancy had been abused. If we hadn't raided the place, he probably would have been euthanized, she said. It took Clancy a whole month to learn to trust us. After that, he became my best friend. I hoped he was okay. I hoped he wasn't too scared.

Chapter Nine

Clancy was thirsty. He was hungry. He was sore. He lay on his side in the dirt, the chain heavy on his neck.

A scent reached him.

Man scent.

A tremor of fear ran through Clancy. It wasn't the same man. It wasn't the sour man. But still, Clancy rolled onto his belly and skulked as far away from the approaching man as the chain would allow. He cringed while waiting to see what the man would do.

The man approached slowly, speaking softly. Clancy wanted to get away from him, but when he pulled back, the chain around his neck tightened.

The man crouched in front of Clancy. He grabbed him by the muzzle and lifted his head. Clancy wanted to resist, but he was afraid to. Besides, so far this man hadn't hurt him.

The man stood up. He walked away. Clancy felt his whole body relax. This man was not like the sour man.

The man came back. He set down a bowl of water and another of food. When Clancy dove for the food, the man did not beat him. Clancy ate with relish. He lapped up the water. He started to feel better. The man scratched Clancy's head when he took away the empty food bowl. He left the water bowl and even added some more water to it. Clancy sank to the ground.

Chapter Ten

A sudden yank on the heavy chain around Clancy's neck almost choked him. He sprang to his feet and lunged forward with the chain to try to loosen it. The man pulled it tighter. He laughed.

It was the sour-smelling man. Just as suddenly as he had yanked the chain, he let it drop to the ground. Clancy gasped for breath.

Something hit him hard on the head.
The sour man was holding a long stick.
The end was wrapped with fabric. The
man poked the stick at Clancy, hitting
him in the muzzle. Clancy lunged
forward and caught the end of it in his
mouth. With its thick cushion of fabric,
it was easy to hold on to. But the man
was strong too. Whenever he got the
stick away from Clancy, he beat him
with it, until all Clancy wanted to do
was kill the stick. Kill the man too, if
he could.

The man with the stick laughed and
walked away.

Clancy quickly learned to watch
for the sour man. He came back often.
He was the one who brought pain. He
was the one who laughed at Clancy.
He poked Clancy and hit him. Clancy
fought back. He grabbed the cloth end
of the stick whenever he could and bit
down hard, until his jaws ached, to hold

it for as long as he could. So Clancy was alert and on his feet when he caught the man's scent again.

The man approached, carrying the big stick. This time the man was not alone. This time he had a brown dog with him. A snarling, growling dog that strained at his chain as soon as he saw Clancy.

The sour man laughed when he poked Clancy with the stick. He laughed again when he let go of the brown dog's chain. The dog raced at Clancy and clamped his jaws around Clancy's muzzle before Clancy had a chance to react. Clancy yowled in agony. He tried to fight back, but the brown dog's jaws stayed clamped on him.

Clancy shook his head furiously, trying to get the brown dog to let go. To his surprise, the other dog's grip loosened and Clancy was able to bite back. But the brown dog rushed him again, biting a hind leg before Clancy

bit down on the first thing he could—
the brown dog's hind quarter. The other
dog yelped and came at Clancy in a
fury. Clancy dodged him once, twice…
and then the two collided in a tangle of
snarling and snapping.

Someone shouted. A hand grabbed
the brown dog's chain and pulled him
off Clancy with a sharp command.
It was the other man, the one who had
given Clancy food. Clancy sank to the
ground and licked his wounds.

The two men argued for a while.
Then the sour man and the dog left, and
the other man came over and crouched
in front of Clancy.

"I figured you for game," he said
to Clancy. "Looks like I wasn't wrong.
We're going to start training you up
tomorrow."

Chapter Eleven

Clancy had been missing for three days now. Dad called the SPCA again to see if anyone had turned in a dog matching Clancy's description. Mom made a new poster, and I stuck that up around town. But so far nobody had seen Clancy. Nobody called.

I was walking along Dundas Street after school. Dundas is a street with a lot of stores and restaurants, so it attracted a lot of pedestrians. I was putting up the new posters on every single utility pole when someone called my name.

It was Gayle.

"How come I had to find out from your friend Ben and not from you?" she asked.

"Find out what?"

"What you found out on the county road. One of your dog's tags. Ben says you agree with me. He said you think it's dognappers. He said you went to the police."

"Not that it did me any good."

"You have to take me there. You have to show me exactly where you found that tag. Maybe there's some clue out there about Pucci."

I stared at her big watery eyes behind her thick glasses. I'd forgotten that her dog was missing too. She probably missed him as much as I missed Clancy.

I told her everything—about finding the tag, talking to the woman at the farmhouse who told me about the dark-blue van, going to the police, the whole story.

"We looked for other clues while we were out there, but we didn't find anything."

"Maybe you missed something," Gayle said. "You don't even know my dog. Maybe there's something there that only I would recognize."

"Like what?"

"I don't know," she said. "But I want to see the place. You have to take me there."

"It won't do any good. And I want to put up these posters."

"Please?" she begged.

"I can't right now. But I can tell you exactly where it is."

She made me draw a map with the two farmhouses on it and an X where we had found the tag.

"I'm going to ride out there and take a look," she said.

I was no longer listening to her. I was staring at what was happening across the street.

A dark-blue van was parked at the curb. Its two back doors were open, and a man who had just come out of a pet store was loading two heavy bags into it. Bags of dog food. He left the van doors open when he went back into the store.

I darted across the street and peeked through the front window of the pet store. The man was leaning against the counter, talking to the girl at the cash.

I slid around the side of the van and looked inside. Besides the two huge bags, there were also cans of dog food. It all added up to one massively hungry dog—or a lot of dogs that needed to be fed. A huge coil of chain sat in one corner of the van, next to a tarp that someone had just tossed in.

Then something caught my eye. Something that glinted on the floor of the van. It was a tiny piece of metal. A loop. The kind of metal loop that holds a dog tag to a dog's collar. Like the one we had found near Clancy's tag. This had to be the van.

I glanced at the store again. The man was sliding his wallet into his jeans pocket. He was coming out. I had to think fast.

Should I call the cops? If I did, what would I say? I had no solid evidence of a crime. All I had was a man buying dog food. The police weren't going to help me without evidence that a crime was being committed.

If the police wanted evidence, it was going to be up to me to get it.

I had to know where this man was going.

I couldn't chase him on foot. And even if I grabbed Gayle's bike from her,

I would lose the van as soon as it accelerated at the town limits. That left me with one choice.

I jumped inside the van and pulled the tarp over me.

The man slammed the doors shut, climbed in behind the wheel and drove off. At first I knew what direction we were going. But the van made so many turns that after a while I lost track. Then suddenly we were going faster and straighter. I was pretty certain we were on the county road.

It wasn't long before the van came to a stop. The man got out and opened the back doors. I heard him slide the two bags of dog food toward him. I waited, listening to the crunch of boots on gravel as he walked away. Then... nothing. I waited a little longer before I peeked out from under the tarp. He was gone, but where and for how long? Five minutes? Five seconds?

I had to get out of the van.

I slipped out from under the tarp and crawled to the van doors. A quick peek outside showed me there was no one out there. At least, no one I could see. The sun was getting low in the sky.

I jumped out of the van. I waited until my heart had stopped pounding before I chanced another quick look around. I saw lights in the distance. Two sets of them. From two farmhouses. The van had stopped at the same place where we had found Clancy's tag. This had to be the right van. I was close to finding the dognappers.

I heard voices and ran for the cover of the culvert where Ben and I had leaned our bikes. There were two people talking, both men. Their voices got closer and closer.

"You should have gone around the other way," one of the men said. "You know how Cal is."

"The other way around takes an extra twenty minutes. Besides, that so-called road is murder on my suspension. If anyone sees me out here, they'll probably think I was taking a leak in the bush."

"If you went around the other way, we could unload this stuff at the shed door. Now I have to schlep it down the trail."

"Stop complaining and grab a crate of cans," the other man said.

I heard the van doors slam. The two men jumped the culvert and headed through the field and into the scrub on the other side of the road. Crouching low and staying well behind them, I followed.

Chapter Twelve

I trailed the two men through scrub that reached my thighs. Beyond that was bush—the end of the fields and the beginning of the woods that stood where nothing else did. The two men disappeared in the trees.

I followed at a distance. The woods were made up mostly of pine, which grew tall and spindly and had all their needles way, way up high, where they fought each other for a piece of sky and their share of the sunlight. It was hard to hide among all those trunks. I had to stay far back.

I followed the men's voices because there wasn't much of a path to follow. The ground was littered with pine needles and fallen branches, rotting logs and outcroppings of rock. The land was uneven, downhill here, uphill there, making it easy to stumble.

It was dark in the woods too. The sun had started to set before I left town. Whatever was left of it wasn't getting through the trees to where I was.

I froze when I heard a loud snap.

"Where are you going?" one of the men asked.

I pressed myself flat against a skinny pine, my heart hammering in my chest again. Had he seen me?

"Where do you think I'm going?" the other man said. "I'm going back to the van. There's only so long a man can pretend to be taking a leak."

"But we're not even halfway there yet."

"So? Get one of your guys to help you."

I heard more snaps and crackles. One of the men was coming back. I scrambled out of the way and threw myself flat behind a rotting log.

The man from the van didn't even try to be quiet as he headed back to the road. He stomped through the woods like Godzilla tromping through Tokyo. When he had passed and I couldn't hear him anymore, I stood up, brushed myself off and tried to find my bearings.

It was darker now, and there were no voices to tell me which direction to take. There were no lights anywhere either.

I dug my cell phone out of my pocket. Should I call my dad and tell him where I was? If I did, he would probably tell me to get out of there and let the police take care of it. But take care of what exactly? I could just imagine the sneer on that cop's face if I told him I had climbed into a stranger's van and followed him because he'd bought dog food and his van was blue. Where's the crime in that? he would ask. The police were only interested in crime. They needed evidence of that, which I didn't have.

I switched off my phone and stuffed it back into my pocket. I walked deeper into the woods.

Finding your way in dark woods you've never been in before can be tricky. For one thing, when you're surrounded by pine trees as far as you can see, and it's dark, and you can't see the sky, everything looks exactly the same. For another, without any clear markers it's easy to lose your sense of direction. I stumbled around in the dark until I didn't know which direction I had come from and which direction I had been going in.

I was still stumbling around when a face appeared in the darkness and a hand clamped over my mouth.

"Relax," Gayle said, "and don't scream."

I shoved her hand away. "I wasn't going to scream." Who did she think she was talking to? "What are you doing here?"

"I saw you jump into that van, Kenzie."

"And you followed me on your bike?"

"Yeah. For a while. Then I lost him. I took a chance. When I got here, I saw the van parked at the side of the road. Then I saw the driver come out of the woods. But I didn't see you anywhere. When the van took off, I decided to come and investigate. So where are we going?"

I told her about the second man who had helped carry the food. "I think he went that way," I said, pointing. But I really wasn't sure at all anymore.

"A man with a lot of dog food headed through these woods?" Gayle thought for a minute. "What if the man in the van and the man who met him out here bought all that dog food to feed the dogs they've been kidnapping?"

"That's exactly what I thought. But I lost them. Now we'll have to start all over again trying to catch them. I should have taken down the van's license plate. Did you get it?"

She didn't answer me.

"If they have a lot of dogs, they're keeping them somewhere," she said.

"They wouldn't buy so much dog food if they weren't keeping lots of dogs," I said.

"Exactly. Come on."

"Where are we going?"

"I may be wrong," Gayle said, "but I think I know where they're headed." She nudged me aside and took the lead. She strode through the woods as if she owned them. I had to scramble to keep up.

Chapter Thirteen

We didn't run into any abandoned dog food along the way, so either we were headed in the wrong direction or the second man had found someone to help him carry the food the rest of the way.

We walked for what seemed like a long time. I got hit in the face by three different branches, tripped over a million tree roots and almost twisted my ankle when my foot broke through a tangle of forest debris that I was trying to climb over.

"Are you sure you know—" I whispered.

"Shhh!"

Gayle had stopped and was staring straight ahead.

A few feet in front of us was a large clearing, surrounded on all sides by trees. A rustic cabin stood in the middle of the clearing. An old RV was parked on one side of it, and two sheds stood on our side. Beside the cabin, lights strung between poles lit what looked like a shallow, empty swimming pool. The same lights also lit up some of the yard around the swimming pool. I saw two treadmills. I also saw what looked like small pens, the kind you might keep sheep or pigs in.

"What is this place?" I asked.

"It used to be an old homestead. You know, from the pioneer days. Kids used to hang out here all the time, right up until the land was bought by some guy from out of town. He put private-property signs everywhere. I heard he shot at a kid once. Said he thought it was an intruder. Nobody ever came out here again."

"You think the guy who owns the place is kidnapping dogs?"

"I think we should go and find out. You good with that?"

I stared at her. She wasn't at all what I'd thought she was like. Kids made fun of her all the time, mostly because of those thick glasses and the way she kept to herself. But she was smart. She was the one who'd figured out that all those other dogs hadn't just wandered away like the cops seemed to think. She had talked to the people who put up lost-dog signs. She had asked questions

and found out that most of the dogs
had disappeared from backyards. So
far she hadn't given up on trying to
find her dog. And now she was ready
to trespass on land owned by someone
not afraid to use a gun. That took guts.

It was also crazy.

"What if he shoots at us?" I asked.

"We're not going to do anything.
We're just going to get closer so we can
see what's going on. Pucci could be in
there. Clancy too. Don't you want to
take a look?"

The clearing wasn't big. The cabin,
the RV and the two sheds took up the
whole center of the space. There were
lights on in the cabin, and a pickup truck
was parked in front of it, so there had to
be someone inside. If the man who had
met the van driver had come from this
cabin, then according to what I had over-
heard in the woods, he wasn't alone.

"What if we're wrong?" I whispered to Gayle. "What if there are no dogs there?"

She shrugged. "If we're wrong, we're wrong. But at least we'll know."

She crept to the edge of the clearing. She looked around and then, keeping low, she ran toward the closest shed.

I felt like a coward, watching her from the sidelines. I ran after her.

We both crouched, panting, behind the shed. Gayle peered around in the gloom.

"This is bad," she said.

"What do you mean?"

"Look over there."

She pointed to a spot behind the cabin, where the treadmills were.

"Yeah? So? Maybe the guy is a fitness fanatic."

"What about those?" she said. She pointed at something else in the yard.

I looked, but I didn't see what she meant.

"Cages. And chains. Lots of them."

"There was a lot of chain in the van too," I said. "Is that important?"

"It is if I'm right."

"Right about what?"

"I think these guys are holding dog fights, Kenzie. I think that's why they're kidnapping dogs."

"*What?* You can't be serious."

"That stuff over there is what people use to train the dogs and build up their strength. They put them on a treadmill. They keep them in heavy chains to build up their upper-body strength. They give them steroids to make them bigger and more aggressive. And that pit we saw, the one that looks like a little swimming pool? I think that's where they hold the actual fights. The spectators stand around the edge and watch. They bet on which dog is going to win and how long it will take. Sometimes they make the dogs fight to the death, Kenzie. The winner is the survivor."

"We have to call the cops," I said. I fumbled in my pocket for my cell phone.

But Gayle was already running in a crouch to the next shed. There was a window in it with light shining through. There were tall weeds and some scrubby bushes behind the shed. Gayle disappeared between a bush and the back of the shed. After a few seconds her head appeared. She crept over to the window and stood up slowly. She looked inside.

I started after her, but something grabbed my foot. Another tree root. I splatted face-first onto the ground. My cell phone flew through the air and landed with a crack somewhere in the darkness. I was getting to my hands and knees when dogs started barking. Lots of dogs.

I stared at Gayle. I waved frantically at her to tell her we had to go. When the men in the cabin heard the dogs barking, they would come to investigate. One of them might come out with his gun. She knew that. She was the one who had told me the story.

But she didn't pay any attention to my warning. Instead, she waved at me to join her.

The cabin door opened. A man appeared, framed in the light from inside. His voice carried to where I lay frozen on the ground.

"They're just worked up," he said. "They can smell what's coming."

"Go and check on them anyway," another voice said. It came from inside the cabin. "I don't want to take any chances. They're going to start arriving any time now."

I scrambled to my feet and ran to Gayle. I grabbed her arm.

"More people are coming," I hissed in her ear. "We have to get out of here."

"There's a chocolate Lab in there."

I raised my head to look through the window just as the door to the shed opened and the man from the cabin walked in. I ducked down again—fast.

When Gayle opened her mouth to say something, I clamped my hand over it and held it there.

The man clomped around inside the shed, which caused more barking. What if he came outside? What if he found us?

"Come on. We have to go *now*," I whispered in Gayle's ear.

Suddenly the whole clearing lit up. Beams of light sliced through the trees. Other noises joined the symphony of barking dogs. The sound of vehicles crunching over gravel, and the shouts of greeting from the new arrivals. Several pickup trucks and vans swung around to park on the scrubland behind the cabin and the sheds. I grabbed Gayle and yanked her down behind the shed.

More vehicles filled the clearing. The people in them—mostly men, judging by their voices—stood around, headlights still on, popping open cans of beer. They blocked our path to the safety of the woods.

We were trapped.

Chapter Fourteen

Gayle and I made ourselves as small as we could in our tiny hiding space between the shed and the bush. More vehicles arrived. The barking got crazy. Drivers still stood around drinking beer and talking about odds. But that had to change soon. If the men were here for fights, eventually they would gather around the pit. When they moved, Gayle and I could escape.

It seemed to take forever before someone rang a triangle, like a cook in an old Western calling the cowboys to the chuck wagon. Headlights went off one by one until it was finally dark behind the shed. Just as I'd hoped, the men all drifted toward the pit.

I tugged on Gayle's hand, but she didn't stand up.

"I think I saw your dog in there," she said.

My pulse raced. I crept to the window and peeked inside. My heart almost exploded when I saw a face pressed against the metal bars of a crate on the other side of the room. It was Clancy's face. Clancy was here, and he was still alive.

I ducked down beside Gayle. "Do you have a cell phone?" I asked.

"Yes, but it's out of juice. Where's yours?"

"I tripped back there and dropped it." And I didn't want to take any chances trying to find it out there in the dark. That was assuming it wasn't under the wheel of a pickup truck by now. "You have to get out of here right now. You have to get to one of those farmhouses across the road and call the police. You have to go now, Gayle."

"What about you? Aren't you coming with me?"

"I'll be right behind you. But first I'm getting my dog."

Gayle tried to argue with me. She said it would be safer if we both left now. That I could get Clancy back when the police showed up.

If they showed up, I thought bitterly. I didn't trust that cop I'd talked to.

"Go now," I said. "I won't be long. I promise—I'll be right behind you."

She finally agreed. After another careful look around, she ran back to the woods. I circled to the side of the shed. Men were crowded around the pit across the scrubby yard. They were all looking down into it. I heard snarling and growling, and every so often the men shouted, urging the dogs on. It made me sick to think about what was going on down there.

It also made me even more determined to get Clancy out of there.

I watched until I was sure no one was looking my way. Then I slipped into the shed. The dogs were barking, but they had been noisy ever since the spectators started arriving. Nobody seemed concerned about the barking now that the fights had started.

I ran to Clancy's cage and unlatched it.

Clancy lunged at me, and I threw my arms around him. It took me a few seconds to see that he had been hurt. There were cuts on his muzzle and dried blood around the uneven stitches someone had given him to close his wounds.

"Come on, Clancy."

He wobbled when he stood up and then raised one leg and put all his weight on the other three. His left rear leg was hurt. I saw blood on it. That did it.

I took the chains from around Clancy's neck and told him to stay. Then I went to the cage next to Clancy's.

A lot of the dogs were fierce-looking—pit bulls and pit bull mixes, a couple of rottweilers, some German shepherds. There were a couple of small dogs too—a bichon frise and a dachshund. There was no way either of them could take on a pit bull. Why had the kidnappers bothered to take them? *Oh, right.* For sport.

I looked at Clancy again.

"Stay," I said again. "You really have to stay, boy."

Then I started opening all the cages. I was scared at first. I thought maybe the dogs would attack me. So I did it as fast as I could and stepped out of the way even faster. When the dogs came out, most of them ran straight out of the shed. I worked quickly. I didn't want to leave anyone behind.

Outside I heard someone yell, "Hey!"

I shouted at Clancy to come, and I ran out of the shed and toward the woods. I looked over my shoulder. Clancy was barely out of the shed. He was having a hard time running on three legs.

Some men raced to their cars. Headlights flooded the area again. Other men were running all over the place, trying to round up the dogs that were loose.

"Come on, Clancy!" I yelled.

"Hey! Hey!"

Suddenly I was blinded by the light. I hit the ground, fast. A shot rang out, cutting through all the barking.

Someone swore.

"Never mind that," someone else said. "We have to clear out of here. Now!"

Clancy was panting, and I knew he was badly hurt. But he kept running. He stayed behind me all the way to the far edge of the woods. I stopped there and squinted into the distance. There was no van parked at the side of the road. If Gayle was out there somewhere, I didn't see her. I peered into the darkness behind me. I didn't hear anyone thundering through the woods after me. I didn't hear anything at all except my own breathing and my heartbeat. And Clancy panting by my side.

Chapter Fifteen

Gayle met me on the road in front of the farmhouse where the lady had told me about the blue van.

"What did the cops say? Are they coming?"

"I made sure they would," Gayle said. "I called the SPCA hotline first. They called the police. We're supposed to wait here. Did you see Pucci?"

That was when I realized I had never even asked her what kind of dog Pucci was.

"He's a cocker spaniel," she said.

I shook my head. "I didn't see him. Sorry."

I asked the lady in the farmhouse if I could use her phone to call my parents. I told them I had found Clancy and that he was hurt. They said they would be there as soon as they could. My sister came with them.

My mother cried when she saw the dried blood on Clancy. My sister threw her arms around his neck and tearfully told him that she would never leave him alone outside again. My dad's face remained grim long after I told him what Gayle and I had found in the woods.

My dad took pictures of Clancy with his cell phone. Then he bundled Clancy into the backseat of the car and told my mother to take him to the vet.

"Traci can stay with him and keep in touch with me by phone. You can drive back here to pick us up after Kenzie talks to the police."

The lady in the farmhouse invited us in. She made coffee for my dad and offered Gayle and me sodas. The cops showed up about half an hour later. Actually, it was just one cop—the same plainclothes officer I had talked to at the police station. There was a woman with him. She introduced herself as JoAnn Hancock, head of the local SPCA.

The officer didn't apologize for doing nothing the first time I talked to him. He did say, "Good work, kids." Then quickly added, "Not that I approve of people taking the law into their own hands. Especially kids."

"Did you arrest the dognappers?"

"Not yet," he said.

"They fled," Ms. Hancock said. "They do that. Whenever they think the police are about to show up, they take off. They'll set up somewhere else and get word out to their customers."

"Customers? You mean the people who show up to bet on the fights?" Gayle said. "How can they even watch dogs tearing each other apart, let alone bet on it?"

"I wish I knew." She turned to me. "You did a good thing, setting all those dogs free. You made sure they wouldn't be forced to fight. We've already started trying to round them up."

"Have you found a cocker spaniel?" Gayle asked.

"We're still searching the property," Ms. Hancock said.

Gayle wanted to go back to the cabin to look for Pucci herself, but the police officer said, "Absolutely not. That's a crime scene. If we find your animal, we'll notify you. I promise."

My sister called to say that Clancy needed a lot of stitches and some antibiotics, but he was going to be okay.

"They used staples on him," she said. "The vet says it looks like he was in a fight, and someone treated Clancy's wounds by stapling them shut. He says sometimes the dog fighters use superglue on them. Superglue, Dad! Do you believe that?" She was so angry that my dad had to hold the phone away from his ear. That's how I heard everything she said.

My mom came back with the car, and we drove Gayle home. We picked up Clancy and my sister at the vet, and then we all went home.

My dad talked to the police the next day. They'd found a lot of dead dogs buried on the property. The SPCA said they were dogs that had lost fights and other, smaller dogs whose sole purpose was to bait and be killed by a fighting dog in training.

Gayle called me two days later. Ms. Hancock had dropped by her house. They had found what they thought was a cocker spaniel among the dead dogs. "She isn't positive it's Pucci, but she said it's the only cocker spaniel they found. There was no collar and no tags, and she says the body is pretty badly decomposed." I could hear her crying softly on the other end of the line.

I told her I was sorry. "I wish we'd found Pucci too," I said.

"Well, I'm glad we found the other dogs, and I'm glad you let them all go."

"What's going to happen to all those dogs?" I asked. "They're all killers."

"Not all of them," Gayle said. "Clancy isn't."

"That's because they didn't have him long enough. Ms. Hancock says if someone decides a dog is good enough to fight, they train them for about six weeks. She says that's what turns them into aggressive animals. They use drugs on them."

"They'll do their best with the aggressive dogs. But some of the dogs have been returned to their owners, Kenzie. That's good."

"Yeah." I didn't really know what else to say. Clancy was home safe, but Pucci was never coming home. I mumbled a lame "Well, guess I'll see you at school" and hung up the phone.

Chapter Sixteen

The house was silent when Clancy struggled to his feet and climbed out of his basket in the kitchen. He padded up the steps, still being careful to keep the weight off his sore foot. When he got to the top of the stairs, he nudged open the first door he saw. He crossed the thick carpet to the bed and jumped up as lightly as he could. Kenzie was curled up under his blanket. His breathing was gentle and even. Clancy lay down next to Kenzie's warm body. He inhaled the boy's familiar scent, as well as the fragrance of the sheets. The bed was soft under his aching body. For the first time in days, he felt completely content.

Norah McClintock won the Crime Writers of Canada's Arthur Ellis Award for crime fiction for young people five times. She wrote more than sixty YA novels, including several for Orca Soundings, and contributed to The Seven Prequels, Seven (the series), The Seven Sequels and the Secrets series.

Titles in the Series

orca soundings

orca soundings

For more information on all the books
in the Orca Soundings series, please visit
www.orcabook.com.